Moore Farm

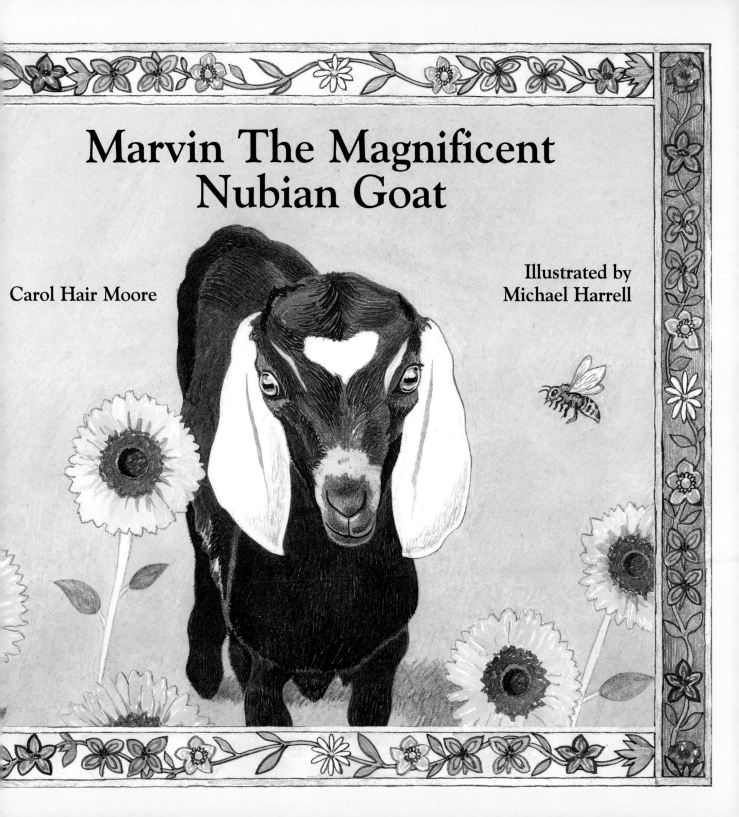

Marvin The Magnificent
Nubian Goat

Carol Hair Moore

Illustrated by
Michael Harrell

To order additional copies of this book: Order online: www.iwishyouicecreamandcake.com
Phone orders: (850) 893-1514
Series: I Wish You Ice Cream and Cake Book I

Inquiries should be addressed to:
CyPress Publications
P.O. Box 2636
Tallahassee, Florida 32316-2636
http://cypresspublications.com | lraymond@nettally.com

Library of Congress Cataloging-in-Publication Data

Moore, Carol Hair, 1940-
    Marvin the magnificent Nubian goat / Carol Hair Moore ;
[illustrations by Michael Harrell]. -- 1st ed.
        p. cm. -- (I wish you ice cream and cake ; bk. 1)
    Summary: A baby farm animal discovers that he is a Nubian goat.
    ISBN 978-1-935083-03-0 (hardcover)
    [1. Nubian goat--Fiction. 2. Goats--Fiction. 3. Domestic
animals--Fiction.] I. Harrell, Michael, ill. II. Title.
    PZ7.M7824Mar 2009
    [E]--dc22
                                    2008050941

ISBN: 978-1-935083-03-0
First Edition

NANA REMINDS US:

THE DOOR IS ALWAYS OPEN.
THE LIGHT IS ALWAYS ON.
THE BED IS ALWAYS MADE.

Carol Hair Moore

This is the story of Marvin's glorious discovery
that he was a magnificent Nubian goat.
Marvin came to live on Moore Farm
when he was five days old.

No other goats were on the farm, and Marvin soon thought the Moores were his family.

"Oh dear, oh dear, I can't stand on two legs like the Moores. I must not be a person."

"What can I be?"

"Maybe I'm a peacock. Mrs. Peacock,
may I join you for lunch?" asked Marvin.

Marvin had a hard time trying to catch bugs.
He knew he wasn't a peacock.

"Maybe I'm a horse, but I don't know how to neigh," exclaimed Marvin.

"Maybe I'm a kitty." Marvin couldn't get throug[h] the small cracks, and he didn't like drinking milk[.]

"Maybe I'm a chicken, but I don't have feathers."

"A cow, a kitty,
a chicken,
a peacock?"

"Oh dear, what am I?"

He drank cool water from the frog pond, and saw his reflection in the peaceful water.

As he looked up, he saw a beautiful Nubian goat coming toward him.
He was a very large goat.

The Nubian goat came to visit Moore Farm that glorious crisp day.
The Moores' cousins, the Langs, had a neighboring farm.
They brought their goat over for a visit with Marvin.

At first glance, Marvin thought he saw himself,
but the visiting goat was much bigger than Marvin.

Marvin realized that
he was a goat.

"I am a goat!"
he exclaimed.

"Now I can just
be me. There is
nothing better
than to just
be me."

Moore Farm

Carol, presenting **Marvin the Magnificent Nubian Goat**
to the Florida Governors Mansion Library. It is read to the visiting children.

Carol was born in Live Oak, a small north Florida town halfway between Tallahassee and Jacksonville. Her ancestors arrived in the Live Oak area by covered wagon in the 1850s. Much of Carol's early life was spent in a rural environment, during which she developed her love of animals, especially farm animals.

She received her B.S. Degree in Elementary Education from Florida State University and taught second grade in Gainesville, Florida, while her husband Ed obtained his law degree.

Ed and Carol raised their three children on Moore Farm just outside of Tallahassee. While Moore Farm contained many animals including cows, horses, chickens, peacocks, turkeys, cats, dogs, and ducks, the family favorite was Marvin the pet goat. Marvin lived to be twelve years old and was an integral part of the Moore Farm.

Ed and Carol's seven grandchildren love to visit Nana and Dadaddy at their home in Tallahassee and their coast home at Saint Teresa on the Gulf of Mexico.

Illustrator, Michael Harrell

Michael Harrell is a native of Tallahassee, Florida. He received a B.F.A. from the University of Georgia in 1989.

Harrell's seascapes and landscapes paintings can be found in private and corporate collections throughout the U.S. and abroad.

His oils and watercolors have been featured in many national publications, including *American Artist Watercolor* magazine, *American Art Collector*, and *The Artist's Magazine.* More than a dozen top galleries represent Harrell's work and, in 2004, *The Artist's Magazine* listed Michael Harrell as one of the top 20 artists in the United States to watch.

Michael Harrell's clients have included American Express, Paramount Pictures, Seaside, and the Mystic Seaport Museum.

Marvin was a male Nubian goat. Males are called "bucks." The female goats are called "does." The Nubian goat is of oriental origin and is a large goat with long ears lying close to the head. The Nubians come in many colors, solid or patterned, and have short, shiny hair. Nubians are prized for their high butterfat milk production.

You can visit Carol Moore at www.**iwishyouicecreamandcake.com**